Amy Animal Talker

The Mystery Cat

Diana Kimpton

Illustrated by
Desideria Guicciardini

USBORNE

The Clamerkin Clan

Hilton

Amy

Einstein

Plato

Isambard

Willow

Bun

To Ksusha

First published in the UK in 2010 by Usborne Publishing Ltd., Usborne House, 83-85 Saffron Hill, London EC1N 8RT, England. www.usborne.com

Text copyright © Diana Kimpton, 2010

Illustration copyright © Usborne Publishing Ltd., 2010

The right of Diana Kimpton to be identified as the author of this work has been asserted by her in accordance with the Copyright, Designs and Patents Act, 1988.

Cover photograph © Jean-Michel Labat/Ardea.com

The name Usborne and the devices ♀ ⊕ are Trade Marks of Usborne Publishing Ltd.

A CIP catalogue record for this book is available from the British Library.

First published in America in 2013 AE.

PB ISBN 9780794531492   ALB ISBN 9781601302991

JFMAMJJ SOND/12   00075/1

Printed in Dongguan, Guangdong, China.

CHAPTER ONE

"Oh no!" said Amy Wild, as the wind tore the leaflet from her hand. She tried to grab it, but she was too late. The sheet of paper spun out of her reach and danced away up the road.

"I'll get it," barked the terrier walking beside her. He raced after the escaping leaflet as fast as his short legs could carry him. Then he jumped into the air and caught it between his teeth.

"Thanks, Hilton," said Amy, as she took it from his mouth. The leaflet was soggy and full of teethmarks. But the dog looked so pleased with himself that she didn't like to tell him it was useless.

Instead she said, "I don't think we need to deliver this last one. There's only Mrs. Damson's cottage left and she knows all about the Grand Reopening because I told her at school."

"Did you tell her everything?" asked the Siamese cat crouched in the shelter of the hedge. "Even the name of the mystery celebrity?"

Amy laughed. "Of course I didn't. It's a secret."

"You shouldn't need to ask that, Willow," said Hilton. "You know Amy's really good at keeping secrets. She's never told anyone that she can talk to animals."

"And I've never given the slightest hint that my necklace is magic," added

Amy, as she touched the string of glittering paws that hung around her neck. Her great-aunt, Granty, had given it to her when Amy first came to live on the Island of Clamerkin. And Granty was the only other human in the world who knew that the necklace gave Amy the power to understand everything animals said.

Willow stepped out from under the hedge into the full force of the wind. "Please tell me who the celebrity is," she purred, as she rubbed herself against Amy's legs.

"No," said Amy. "You'll have to wait until tomorrow like everyone else on the Island. You'll find out who it is when you see them open the new, improved Primrose Tea Room."

At that moment, an extra-strong gust of wind tore into them. It made Hilton's hair stand on end and sent Willow scurrying back under the hedge.

Amy hunched her shoulders against the blast and glanced across the fields to the sea. It was wild and gray and streaked with white. "Look how rough it is. I'm glad I'm not out in a boat today."

"I wish I wasn't out at all," mewed Willow.

"Let's go home," Hilton suggested.

Amy was about to agree when something furry crashed into her legs. She looked down and saw Isambard

– the tabby cat from the repair shop. He had been running so hard that he wasn't looking where he was going.

"Come quickly," he panted. "The clan's been called out."

He didn't have to ask twice. The clan was the group of animals that took care of Clamerkin Island and Amy was the only human member. Hilton and Willow belonged too, and they all knew that a call-out meant someone was in trouble.

Isambard raced away up a path between some bushes. The others followed at top speed. It was easy to run with the wind behind them. Amy felt as if she was being blown along.

Suddenly the tabby cat dived under

a fence. Willow and Hilton sped after him. But Amy couldn't. She was too big to slide underneath so she had to climb over the top. As a result, she was the last to reach the tree on the far side of the field.

The strong wind had blown it over. Now the tree lay on its side like a helpless giant with green hair. Two more members of the clan were waiting beside it – Einstein, the white Persian from the school, and Bun, the fat black cat with white paws who lived at the bakery.

"That's everyone," said Isambard. "Plato's not coming. He says it's too stormy for flying."

Amy wondered if Granty's parrot was just making excuses. Then a sparrow took off from the fallen tree and tried to fly toward her. As he flapped his wings as hard as he could, Amy saw that Plato was right. The wind was too strong. The tiny sparrow couldn't fly against it. Then an extra-large gust caught him and tossed him backward into the leafy branches.

Amy rushed over to see if he was alright. As she peered closely at the motionless bird, another sparrow hopped anxiously toward the same place. "Dear oh dear," she twittered. "Are you alright, Alf?"

The mention of his name made Alf sit up and fluff out his feathers. "Don't worry, Gladys." He nodded his head toward Amy. "Everything's going to be fine now that the Talker is here."

Amy stared at him in confusion. "What's so special about me?"

"You've got hands," replied Alf.

Isambard looked wistfully at his own paws. "Wonderful things — hands — especially in a situation like this."

"Which is getting worse by the minute," cried Gladys, as she jumped anxiously up and down on the fallen tree. "If you don't hurry, my babies are going to die."

CHAPTER TWO

Amy felt a wave of panic. The sparrows were relying on her, but she didn't know what to do. She bent down until her face was close to Gladys and spoke as calmly as she could. "I can't help unless you tell me what's happened."

"It's all our fault," sobbed the mother bird. "We should have known this tree was the wrong place to build a nest."

Amy was puzzled. "I thought nests and trees go naturally together?"

"Not for sparrows like us," explained Alf. "Generations of Clamerkin sparrows have built their nests in hedges. But that wasn't good enough for us. We wanted to be different. We wanted to live in a tree."

"And now look what's happened," said Gladys. "Our nest's overturned and all our poor babies have tumbled out. If we don't rescue them soon, they'll die of cold."

"Don't worry, I'll save them," cried Amy, as she finally understood why her hands were so important. Without them, the birds couldn't pick up the fallen babies or move the nest to safety.

"I'll show you where they are," tweeted Alf. He hopped into the mound of leaves that had once been the top of the tree and Amy started to follow him.

As soon as she pushed her head between the branches, she noticed how much quieter it was inside the tree. The roar of the wind was muffled by the leaves. She listened hard, trying to hear the high-pitched tweeting of the baby birds. But she couldn't. Instead, she heard another sound – a much deeper one.

"What was that?" she asked, as she pulled her head out of the tree again.

Hilton and the cats stared at her with puzzled expressions. So did Gladys.

"What are you talking about?" asked Einstein.

"That noise," said Amy.

"I didn't hear anything," said Willow. The others shook their heads.

"You must have," said Amy. "It sounded like someone groaning."

"Perhaps it was Bun's tummy rumbling," suggested Isambard.

The black cat looked thoughtful. "I suppose it might have been. I didn't notice it myself, but I am feeling a little hungry."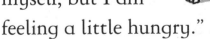

"That's no surprise," said Willow. "You're always hungry."

Amy knew that was true, but she wasn't sure it explained the sound she had just heard. That was much more of a groan than a rumble, and it hadn't seemed to come from Bun's direction. But there wasn't time to solve the mystery now. She had to rescue the baby sparrows first.

"Come on," called Alf from inside the tree.

Amy climbed in after him. But it wasn't easy. The fall had pushed the branches even closer together than they would have been when the tree was upright. She had to wiggle and push to squeeze between them. And she had to be careful where she put her feet. She didn't want to stand on a baby bird by mistake.

Luckily she didn't have to go far before she reached the nest. She was glad she had Alf to show her where it was. The neatly woven bundle of twigs blended so perfectly with its surroundings that she would have found it hard to see by herself.

The nest lay upside down, balanced on two branches. Amy lifted it carefully. To her disappointment, there were no baby sparrows hidden underneath. So she turned the empty nest right side up and looked around for its missing occupants.

"I'll call them," said Alf. He puffed out his chest and sang, "Daddy's here."

Immediately a chorus of high voices

twittered in response. "Feed me, feed me," they called.

"That's a good idea," moaned a deeper voice.

Amy pushed her head out of the tree and glared at Bun. "I'm trying to concentrate. Stop talking about food."

The black cat looked surprised. "I wasn't. I was only thinking about it. I didn't know you could hear me think."

Neither did Amy. But she put the puzzle out of her mind for the time being and went back to her search. "Feed me, feed me," demanded the babies. With Alf's help, she followed the sounds of their voices and found them scattered among the leaves below where the nest had fallen.

One by one, she picked up the shivering babies and popped them back in their nest. Soon they were all snuggled cozily together again and loudly demanding food. Their desire to eat seemed more important to them than anything else.

"Aren't they beautiful?" said Alf, when they were all warm and safe again.

Amy looked hard at the babies. They were too young to have any feathers, and their gaping mouths looked ridiculously big compared to their skinny bodies. Beautiful wasn't a word she would have used to describe them. But she didn't want to hurt the sparrow's feelings, so she smiled and

nodded her
agreement.
Then she
picked up
the nest and
climbed carefully
out of the tangle of
branches into the full force of the wind.

"I told you she'd do it," Alf shouted
to his wife. Gladys hopped onto Amy's
arm and added her thanks to his.

"Where do you want your nest now?"
asked Amy.

"In the hedge," declared Gladys.
"We've had enough of being different."

Alf agreed. "From now on we're
going to behave like real Clamerkin
sparrows." He found a suitable spot

and waited while Amy pushed the nest into its new position. Then he and Gladys hopped away to find food for their hungry family. It was still too windy for flying.

"Time to go home then," barked Hilton. All the cats chorused their agreement.

But someone else had other ideas. "What about me?" called the deep voice that Amy had heard before.

This time the others heard it too, and it definitely wasn't Bun. The voice was coming from somewhere under the tree.

CHAPTER THREE

"Is somebody there?" Amy called, as she bent down beside the fallen tree.

"Of course there is!" came the reply from somewhere under the mound of branches. "If I wasn't here, I wouldn't be talking to you."

Hilton put his head under the leaves and sniffed deeply. "Smells like a cat to me. A very scared cat."

"Having a dog around won't make him feel any calmer," said Willow. She pushed the terrier out of the way and shoved her own head under the leaves instead. "Who are you?" she asked.

There was a long pause. Then the voice said, "That's a tricky question."

Isambard gave a snort of disgust. "It doesn't sound very difficult to me."

"Even I know who I am," said Bun. "And I'm not a very clever cat."

"Maybe this one's really silly," suggested Einstein.

"There's no need to be rude!" The owner of the voice sounded offended. "It's not easy to think when you're under a tree."

"Don't worry," said Amy. "We'll get you out."

Isambard shook his head. "I'm not so sure. We'd need a crane to lift that tree."

Amy stared thoughtfully at the branches that held the cat prisoner. "Maybe we don't need to lift the whole thing. Maybe we could just move enough branches out of the way to set him free."

"Great idea," said Hilton. He seized a branch between his teeth and started to pull it backwards. Amy hoped it would snap so they could take it right away. But it didn't. It bent farther and farther.

"Is that as far as it will go?" asked Einstein, when Hilton eventually stopped pulling.

"Mmmm mmm mmm," replied Hilton, through a mouthful of tree.

"What did you say?" asked Einstein.

Hilton opened his mouth to speak more clearly. But doing that made him let go of the branch. It unbent at top speed and sprang back to its original position.

Unfortunately,
Bun had chosen
that moment
to wander over
to the fallen tree.
"Ouch!" he yowled, as
the branch slammed into his backside.

"Sorry," called Hilton. "That wasn't
as good an idea as we thought."

"Maybe Amy should try," said
Willow. "She's got hands."

Amy shook her head. "I don't think
I'd be any better than Hilton."

"A crane would be," said Isambard.
"Wonderful machines — cranes."

"But we don't have one," said Amy.
"We'll have to think of something else."

"I heard a story at school about

some prisoners," said Einstein. "They got out by digging a tunnel."

"I'm not in a good position for digging," said the mystery cat. "Having a tree on top of me means I'm pretty flat."

"So much for that idea," sighed Einstein.

"Not necessarily," said Amy. "If he can't dig out, maybe we can dig in."

"A mechanical digger could do that," said Isambard. "Wonderful machines – mechanical diggers."

"My front paws are pretty good too," said Hilton. "Out of my way, everyone. Let the doggy digger through."

He rushed up to the tree and sniffed deeply to make sure where the cat was trapped. Then he started to scrabble furiously at the ground. Dirt and stones shot backwards between his hind legs. Amy and the cats retreated to a safe distance to avoid being hit by flying debris.

Hilton took no notice of them. He was too busy with his task. He dug so fast that he soon made a hollow under the tree that was big enough for him to wiggle through. He vanished into it until only the tip of his tail could be seen. Then he backed out more slowly, heaving and puffing as he pulled something behind him. It was covered with orange fur and protesting loudly.

"Let go of my tail," yowled the rescued cat.

"Sorry," said Hilton, as he released his grip. "It was the only part of you I could get hold of."

"I suppose that's alright then," moaned the orange cat. He staggered to his feet and looked around at his rescuers. "Thanks for getting me out. Have I met any of you before?"

Amy stared at him in amazement. "Don't you know?"

"If he doesn't, he really is silly," said Einstein.

"Maybe I am," wailed the rescued cat. "I can't remember anything before that tree hit me on the head — not even my own name."

"Oh!" said Willow. "That explains why you wouldn't tell us."

"Maybe it's Marmalade," suggested Bun. "You're the right color."

"You're just thinking of food again," said Isambard. "He could be called anything – Tiddles or Ginger or Tinkerbell or—"

"Stop!" said Amy. "That really isn't helping. Can't you see that it's making him more upset?" She walked over and picked up the orange cat. He was shivering from cold and shock.

Amy stroked him and turned her back to the wind to protect him from the worst of the weather. The storm was getting wilder by the minute. The wind howled even louder than before and the sky was filled with brooding, black clouds.

Willow had noticed the sky too.
"It's going to pour in a minute. Let's
go home."

"I can't," mewed the orange cat.
"I can't remember where it is."

Amy gave him a reassuring hug.
"Don't panic. I'll take care of you. And
after the storm's over, I'm sure we'll
find out who you are." She hoped she
sounded more confident than she felt.
She had never met a cat with a lost
memory before, and she wasn't sure
what she could do to help.

CHAPTER FOUR

Amy trudged home through the storm
with Hilton and Willow beside her. She
carried the orange cat in her arms. It
didn't seem fair to make him walk so
soon after his accident.

"We're here," she said, as they
reached the Primrose Tea Room. But
the cat didn't reply. He was fast asleep.

The Primrose looked much neater

than it had six weeks ago when Amy first came to live there. Mom and Dad had worked hard since then, trying to turn Granty's run-down business into one that could support them all. They had redecorated the whole place, inside and out, and bought brand-new cups and saucers.

Beside the freshly-painted front door hung a poster printed in green on primrose yellow paper.

The sight of the poster reawakened Willow's curiosity. She paused before heading back to the Post Office and asked, "Is the celebrity that actress, Tina Truelove?"

"No," said Amy and immediately wished she hadn't. If she kept telling

people when they were wrong, what
would she do if someone guessed right?

"How about Craig Redmile?"
suggested Willow. "I love his music."

This time Amy was more careful. She smiled at the Siamese cat and said, "I'm not saying."

"Is it James Dark – the one in all those secret agent films?"

"She's not saying," Hilton reminded Willow.

The cat stuck her tail in the air and turned her back on him. Then she continued with her questioning. "It's not that amazing football player, is it? The one who's married to a singer?"

"Please stop," said Amy. "It's a secret, and it's going to stay that way until tomorrow." But deep down inside, she felt a twinge of anxiety. Everyone Willow suggested was world-famous, but the person coming to open the

Primrose was much less well known. Would everyone be disappointed when they found out who the mystery celebrity really was?

At that moment, a flash of lightning tore across the sky and the first drops of rain plummeted down. One landed on Willow's head and sent her running for home.

Hilton ran too and so did Amy. She was still carrying the lost cat. He woke up as they raced down the path beside the Primrose and in through the back door. Amy breathed deeply, enjoying the welcoming warmth and the delicious smell of baking.

The cat did the same. "I like it here," he said.

"Thank goodness you're back," said Mom, as they stepped into the kitchen. "I would never have let you go out delivering leaflets if I'd known the weather was going to be this bad."

"But I'm glad you did," said Dad. "We need as much publicity as we can get."

"And I'm sure you were safe with Hilton to take care of you," said Granty, who was cutting up a tray of freshly-cooked lemon cake. She held out a piece to Amy and suddenly noticed the orange cat in her arms. "Who do you have there?" she asked.

"I found him. He was trapped under a fallen tree and Hilton helped him get out."

"Very nice, dear," said Mom, as she washed the last mixing bowl and stacked it on the draining board. "But I don't see why you brought him here."

"He's got nowhere else to go. He's lost." Amy chose her words carefully. She didn't want to give away the fact that he'd been talking to her. The necklace's magic powers had to stay secret, even from Mom and Dad.

"That's very sad," said Dad. "But it's the Grand Reopening tomorrow and that's more important. We have to make a success of it, and there's still lots to do." He picked up a tray of primrose yellow cups and saucers and carried it toward the door. "I've still got all these to put behind the counter and we've got to unpack the glasses and set the tables and goodness knows what else. We can't cope with a stray cat as well."

Mom nodded her agreement. "He can't stay here. He's unhygienic." Then she picked up another tray of cups and followed Dad out of the kitchen.

Amy looked pleadingly at Granty, but the old lady shook her head. "It's not my decision. Your mom and dad run the Tea Room now and I promised not to interfere."

The orange cat huddled down in Amy's arms as if he was trying to hide.

"Please don't send me out in that storm again," he mewed.

Granty couldn't understand what he was saying, but she knew that Amy could. She made sure that Mom and Dad were safely out of earshot. Then she asked, "Can't he tell you where he comes from?"

Amy shook her head. "He's lost his memory. He can't remember anything, not even his own name."

"Poor old thing," said Granty, as she tickled the cat's ears. "I wish I could help, but I mustn't break my promise. And that's what I'd be doing if I asked your mom and dad to change their minds."

"Then I'll have to do it myself," said Amy. She couldn't let the cat down now.

He was so lost and so lonely. Somehow she had to persuade her parents to let him stay.

She carried the cat out of the kitchen. Then she pushed open the swinging door at the end of the hall and stepped into the public part of the Primrose. The Tea Room's freshly-painted woodwork and primrose-yellow walls made it look bright and welcoming. But Dad was right. There was still plenty to do before tomorrow. A stepladder stood in one corner, all the shelves in the serving area needed to be filled and the new curtains were draped over a chair, waiting to be hung up.

Dad was busy cleaning the sink in the mini-kitchen behind the counter.

Mom was standing in front of the gleaming new tea and coffee machine with an instruction book in one hand. "Press button A," she muttered to herself. "I wonder if that's this one." She pushed a knob and jumped back in surprise as a jet of steam whooshed out.

Amy jumped too and so did the cat in her arms. But Dad stayed calm. He waved his dishcloth toward a white lever at the far end of the machine. "That might be the right one," he suggested.

Mom pressed it and the machine purred into life. Boiling water gushed out of a spout into the waiting teapot. "Perfect," she said. Then she looked up at Amy as if she'd just realized she was there. "Isn't this wonderful? It's the very latest technology."

"I suppose so," said Amy. "But I didn't come to look at that. I came to talk about this cat."

Dad stared disapprovingly at the animal in her arms. "We already told you he's got to go. We can't risk him causing trouble."

"I don't see why he should," said Amy. "We've got Hilton and Plato and they're no trouble."

Dad sighed. "That's because Granty's taught them how to behave. And they're not cats."

"Cats are always a problem," said Mom. "They jump on tables and lick plates and leave dirty footprints everywhere."

"This one won't," said Amy. "I won't let him."

"And my feet aren't dirty," grumbled the cat, in a slightly offended voice. He gave his paws a quick lick to make absolutely sure.

"What a noisy animal," said Mom.

She hadn't understood what he said, but she had heard him meow. "It's almost as if he knows that we're talking about him."

Amy resisted the urge to tell her that he did. Instead, she pleaded, "Please let him stay, just for tonight. I'll take care of him and I promise he won't be a problem."

She clutched the cat tightly as she waited for them to make up their minds. Outside the weather was worse than ever. Thunder crashed overhead and a huge gust of wind rattled the front door on its hinges. Surely they wouldn't make her throw him out into that storm?

CHAPTER FIVE

There was a long pause. Amy bit her lip anxiously while Mom and Dad whispered quietly to each other. They looked at the cat and then at the door. Finally, they made their decision.

"Alright," said Dad. "He can stay for the time being. But it's up to you to make sure he behaves."

Amy grinned. "He'll be perfect.

I'll make sure of that."

"I hope so," said Mom, "because if he does do anything wrong, he'll have to go." She turned back to the tea and coffee machine and picked up the instruction book again.

Amy decided to take the cat into the living room where he would be safely out of the way. She found that Hilton was already there, busy telling Plato about the rescue.

"So this is the mysterious cat," squawked the parrot, as he peered at the new arrival. "Funny color. He looks like a furry orange."

"There's no need to be rude," said the cat. He jumped out of Amy's arms and padded over to the television. It was on as usual – Plato loved watching it.

"How strange," said the cat, as he stood on his hind legs and peered at the screen. "They must be very small people to fit in there." Then he ran behind the TV and sniffed at the wires coming out of the back. "How do they get in and out?"

"Don't be silly," said Plato. "There aren't really any people. They're just pictures on the screen."

"Haven't you seen a television before?" asked Hilton.

The cat shrugged. "If I have, I've forgotten."

Plato tipped his head to the side and asked, "Can you really not remember anything?"

"Nothing at all," the cat replied. "Not even my name."

The parrot scratched his head with his left foot. "We'll have to call you something."

"How about Mystery?" suggested Amy. "It suits you perfectly because it's a mystery where you came from and it's a mystery who you are."

"I like that," said the newly-named cat. "It sounds daring and adventurous. And that's exactly how I feel." He bounded onto the mantelpiece and sniffed a china angel. "Strange. No smell." He licked it. "No taste either." He pushed it with his paw. "Look! It moves."

Amy jumped forward and caught

the angel just before it hit the ground. She put it back in position with one hand and lifted the cat down with the other. "You mustn't go up there," she said firmly.

"Okay," said Mystery and he jumped onto the windowsill instead. He pushed his nose into an empty vase and tipped it over. Amy caught that too and the candle he knocked over next.

"Stop it," she scolded, as she picked him up. "You've got to calm down."

"I can't," said the cat. "There's so much to explore."

"Butter!" said Plato. "That's what you need. I saw a program on TV about moving a cat to a new home, and they recommended putting butter on his paws."

"What for?" asked Hilton.

"It makes the cat sit quietly and lick it off. By the time he's finished, he'll be used to his new surroundings."

"Don't be silly," said Mystery. "I'm not that foolish."

Amy suspected he was right. But she

didn't have any other ideas so it was worth a try. She tucked the orange cat under her arm and headed for the kitchen. It was empty. That was good. She wouldn't have to explain what she was doing to anyone.

She got a knife, cut a lump of butter off the slab in the fridge and rubbed it on Mystery's paws. But it was too cold and hard. It wouldn't stick.

The cat looked pleased. "I told you it wouldn't work."

Amy kept trying and the warmth of her hand gradually softened the butter. Soon all four of Mystery's paws were coated with a thick layer.

"Yuck," said the cat. "That's disgusting. I have to wash."

Amy grinned, but she decided not to say anything. She couldn't risk changing his mind. She carried Mystery back to the living room. Then she spread some newspaper in front of the fire to keep the floor clean and put him in the middle of it. This time the cat didn't run off exploring. He settled down and started to lick off the butter.

"I told you that would work," said Plato. "Now we just need to find out who he is."

"Someone might recognize him at the reopening tomorrow," Hilton suggested. "There'll be lots of people there because they all want to find out who the mystery celebrity is."

"So do I," squawked Plato, hopping

from one foot to the other in excitement. "I'd love it if it was one of those people from local TV. I love watching them. The lady who reads the news is fantastic and that weatherman's got the most amazing hair."

"Don't be silly," said Hilton. "It's sure to be someone more important than any of them."

Amy listened anxiously. Hilton was just like Willow. He was expecting someone really famous. Was everyone else on the Island the same? Would Plato be the only one who wasn't disappointed when they discovered who the celebrity was?

To her relief, Hilton changed the subject. "I think I'll take a nap.

All that digging has worn me out."
He stretched out on the carpet,
closed his eyes and was soon snoring
gently.

Amy sat down on the sofa. The cat
looked very settled now and completely
occupied with washing his paws. It
should be safe to watch TV as long as
she checked on him regularly.

The first time she checked, he was
still washing.

The second time she checked, he was
still washing.

The third time she checked, he wasn't
there at all.

"Oh no," cried Amy, as she jumped
to her feet. "I should have shut the
door." She raced into the hall and

discovered that the cat wasn't very good at cleaning his paws – a trail of buttery paw prints led into the kitchen. She followed them and found Mystery sitting on the counter top. He was busy lapping up milk from the bottle he'd knocked over. The rest of the milk was trickling over the edge into a puddle on the floor.

Amy was just about to chew him out when she heard Dad's footsteps outside. A shiver of fear ran down her back. If he discovered how badly Mystery was behaving, he'd be sure to throw the cat out.

CHAPTER SIX

Amy ran into the hall and stepped quickly between Dad and the paw prints. "How are things going?" she asked, trying not to let her panic show.

"Really well. Granty's helping Mom set the tables so I've come to put the pizza in the oven for supper."

"I can do that," said Amy. "You go back and get on with what you were doing." She pushed Dad back along the hall and waited until he'd disappeared through the door again. Then she went back into the kitchen.

The situation was even worse than before. While she was out of the room, Mystery had tipped over a jar of strawberry jam.  Now he was using his front paws to mix its contents with the milk.

"Look! Red and white make pink. This is fun."

"No, it isn't. It's naughty. Just look at the mess you've made."

"I'm sorry," said Mystery in an unconvincing way. He jumped down from the table, ran over to Amy and rubbed himself against her legs. In the process, he added a trail of pink paw prints to the buttery ones that were already there.

"No, no, no!" Amy grabbed Mystery before he could get into more trouble. She held him carefully with his sticky feet pointing away from her. Then she carried the protesting cat to the sink and washed his paws.

"No!" he wailed. "Cats don't like water. I remember that."

"You should have remembered to behave better," said Amy. She shook the drips off his feet and gently patted his paws dry with a towel. "Do you want to go back out in the storm?"

"No," whispered Mystery, looking genuinely sorry for his behavior. "I won't cause any more trouble. I promise."

"I hope so," said Amy, as she put the cat into an empty laundry basket. "Now stay there and don't move while I clean up this mess."

She started by putting the pizza in the oven. Then she washed the counter top, mopped up the milk and the paw prints and set the table for supper. The work took her much longer than it should have because she had to keep stopping to put the cat back in the laundry basket. He only seemed capable of being good for thirty seconds at a time.

She just managed to finish before Mom, Dad and Granty came in for supper. They looked very relaxed and happy. The preparations were almost finished, and it looked as if the Grand Reopening was going to be a huge success. Only Amy was on edge. How could she make sure Mystery behaved while everyone was in the kitchen?

Luckily, Granty produced a can of sardines to keep him quiet while the humans ate. "It's the only one I have. I'll leave some money on the dresser so you can buy some cat food in the morning."

Amy kept one eye on the cat while

she munched her pizza. He crouched down by his bowl for a surprisingly long time and concentrated on eating. But when all the sardines were gone, he looked around for more food.

First, he headed toward Hilton's bowl. The dog swiftly blocked the way and gave a warning growl. Next, Mystery jumped on Amy's lap. He stretched one front leg over the edge of the table and tried to grab her last piece of pizza. Amy pushed the paw down quickly before Dad noticed it. Then she pushed the cat onto the ground. She couldn't risk him trying that trick again.

Mystery marched over to the trash can. He stood on his back feet, peered

inside and tried to pull out the empty
sardine can. The trash can started to tip.

Mom and Dad went on chatting,
unaware of what was happening
behind them. But Amy knew that
situation wouldn't last long. The trash
can was leaning farther and farther.
She had only seconds to act before it
came crashing down.

CHAPTER SEVEN

"I think I'll go to bed early," Amy announced, as she jumped to her feet and headed for the trash can. She reached it just as Mystery pulled it over and managed to catch it before it hit the ground. Then she picked up the cat and carried him out of the kitchen.

The storm was more noticeable up in her attic bedroom. The wind howled around the house and whistled down the chimney. Rain hammered on the slate roof and beat against the window.

Amy shivered. This was the worst weather she could ever remember. Then she yawned. She had only come upstairs to keep the cat out of trouble. But now that she was here, she realized how tired she was. She was worn out from delivering all those leaflets, rescuing the baby sparrows and cleaning up after the cat.

She put on her pajamas, climbed into bed and turned off the light. Then she snuggled down under her quilt and pulled it up to her chin.

Suddenly, Mystery jumped onto the end of the bed. "Is it time to go to sleep?"

"Of course it is. It's dark."

"That's not a problem for me, of course. Cats see better in the dark than humans."

"You won't if you close your eyes. Now go to sleep." Amy rolled over on her side. In the process, she moved her left foot.

Mystery pounced on it. Amy moved her other foot. Mystery pounced on that too. "I like this game," he said.

"I don't," said Amy. "I'm tired and I want to go to sleep. Now settle down and get comfortable."

She expected the cat to curl up on the end of the bed. But he didn't. Instead he padded across the quilt and lay down beside her. Then he put his two front paws on her shoulder and started

to press them up and down, one after
the other, in a rhythmic motion – left,
right, left, right, left, right...

"Why are you doing that?" she
asked.

"I can't remember," replied Mystery.
"I think it's something I learned to do
as a kitten."

"I wish you'd forgotten that too.
Please stop!"

"If you insist," said Mystery. He

moved away from her shoulder and sat on her head.

Amy sighed. This was going to be a long night. She pushed Mystery away and pulled the pillow over her ears to block out the noise of the storm. She was sure she wouldn't manage to sleep, but eventually she was too tired to stay awake any longer.

Amy was so tired that she slept late. When she finally woke up, it was half past eight. The wind was still blowing strongly, but the worst of the storm had passed. A beam of sunlight shone through the gap between the curtains onto Mystery. He was fast asleep on the quilt, exhausted from working so hard at keeping her awake.

Amy bounded out of bed, full of excitement. This was the big day. In less than two hours, the Grand Reopening would finally be under way. She left Mystery where he was, shut the door firmly to make sure he didn't escape and ran downstairs to see how the final preparations were going.

As soon as she reached the kitchen, she realized something was terribly wrong. Mom, Dad and Granty were sitting around the table looking completely miserable.

Dad looked up at Amy and sighed. "The ferry's not running. It's too windy."

"Why's that a problem? We don't want to go anywhere."

"But the weatherman does," wailed Mom. "Local TV isn't that local. He has to come over from the mainland."

Amy groaned. The local TV weatherman was the mystery celebrity that everyone was waiting to see. She was already worried that he wasn't famous enough to please the crowd. But now the situation was even worse. He wasn't coming at all. No ferry meant no celebrity.

"What are we going to do?" she asked. "Everyone on the Island wants to see who the mystery celebrity is. That's the main reason they're coming to the reopening."

"I know." Dad put his head in his hands and sighed. "It won't be as good if Mom or Granty cuts the ribbon."

Suddenly, Mom brightened up. "Maybe we could find someone else to open the Primrose. No one except us would know it wasn't the person we originally planned to have."

"Fantastic," said Dad. He scratched his head thoughtfully. "I wonder if the principal from the school would do it."

"You can't ask him!" cried Amy. "He's not a celebrity."

"He is important on the Island," said Mom.

"But not important enough," added Granty. She stood up and started to fill the kettle. "Now let's have breakfast while we think what we should do. We'll all feel better after something to eat."

Her words reminded Amy about the lack of cat food. So she grabbed the money from the dresser and set off for the tiny supermarket up the road. When she arrived, she found it was packed with people. They were all trying to guess who the mystery celebrity might be. To Amy's dismay, everyone was expecting someone world-famous.

"I think it might be the Queen," said old Mrs. Arnold as she went out of the door.

Amy bit her lip nervously. The situation was getting worse by the minute. People would be even more disappointed if that idea spread.

She went on worrying while she chose two cans of cat food for Mystery. But when she went to pay, she noticed something that made her forget all about the mystery celebrity. It was a large poster pinned to the wall beside the cash register.

"A lady brought that in earlier," said the girl at the checkout. "She's from one of the boats that are sheltering from the storm. I felt so sorry for her – she looked really upset."

Amy was sure there couldn't be two lost orange cats on the Island. The poster must be about Mystery. If she hurried, she would have time to take him home before the Grand Reopening. That would make sure he couldn't do any more damage.

She abandoned the cat food and ran back to the Primrose as fast as she could. There was a wide red ribbon across the front door, and there were already two people waiting to see who would cut it. One of them was old Mrs. Arnold. She was holding a small flag on a stick, ready to wave at the Queen.

Amy raced down the side path to the back door and up to her room. She grabbed the orange cat from her bed and ran downstairs again. She was in such a hurry that she didn't notice Granty and Hilton in the hall. "Sorry," she said, as she bumped into them.

"I found out who Mystery is. I'm taking him home."

"You'll have to be quick," said Granty. "You don't want to miss the ceremony."

"I won't," said Amy. Then she hurtled out again, with Hilton beside her and the cat in her arms. They had to slow down when they reached the cobbled street because there were so many people walking toward the Primrose. The sight of them reawakened Amy's worries. Was the reopening going to be a disaster? Who *was* going to cut the ribbon?

CHAPTER EIGHT

Amy and Hilton weaved in and out of the crowd as they made their way downhill toward the shore. Suddenly Mystery sniffed the air. "I can smell the sea," he said.

"Can you remember what it is?" asked Amy in surprise.

"Lots of water, very deep. Goes up and down a little all the time and a lot in a storm." The cat stopped and looked thoughtful. "Sleeping was good for me. I seem to be remembering things today."

"Do those things include a yacht called *Random Beat*?" asked Amy.

Mystery shook his head. "That doesn't mean anything yet."

When they reached the bottom of the hill, they could see how rough the sea was. Huge waves roared across the beach and smashed onto the sea wall, sending up clouds of spray. No wonder the ferry hadn't sailed this morning.

The harbor was the only calm spot. It was protected from the waves by a tall breakwater and it was packed full. Amy recognized the local boats. But there were many others she had never seen before, huddling in the shelter of the harbor to escape the full force of the storm.

Mystery perked up when he saw the boats. "I remember now. That's my home over there." He pointed his paw toward a magnificent yacht that was larger than any of the others. It was gleaming white with a tall mast and the words *Random Beat* painted on the side in gold lettering.

Amy walked along the edge of the harbor until she reached the spot where the yacht was tied up. Then she hesitated. There was no bell to ring and no door to knock on, but it didn't seem right to walk onto the deck without being invited. So she stood as close as she could and shouted, "Hello!" The wind snatched the word away before anyone could hear. Amy tried again and again, louder each time.

She was on the point of giving up when a tall, young woman climbed out onto the deck, wearing jeans and a thick sweater. She gave a squeal of delight when she saw the orange cat. "Marmalade! You're safe."

"Bun guessed your name right!" barked Hilton.

"I remember it now," said the orange cat. "It's good to be home." He jumped down from Amy's arms, bounded onto the yacht and rubbed himself against the woman's legs.

She picked him up and gave him a hug. Then she leaned into the cabin and called, "Our naughty cat's back, Craig."

There was the sound of running footsteps. Then a tall man bounded through the cabin door, shouting, "Marmalade!"

Amy's mouth dropped open in astonishment. This wasn't just any person. This was Craig Redmile, the rock star who had had more number one hits last year than any other singer. He was so famous that everyone she knew had heard of him – even Mom and Dad and Willow.

He smiled at her as he stepped off his yacht. "You're amazing. Trish and I thought we'd lost Marmalade for good.

He ran off yesterday, just after we came into the harbor."

"Where did you find him?" asked Trish, as she joined Craig on the shore.

Amy swallowed hard to calm her nerves. "He was trapped under a fallen tree." She pointed at Hilton and added, "My dog dug him out."

"So we have you to thank as well," said Craig, as he bent down and patted Hilton's head. Hilton stared at him with huge, adoring eyes. He obviously recognized Craig too, and he was completely star-struck.

Trish beamed at them both. "I think you deserve a reward." She reached into her pocket, pulled out several bills and pushed them into Amy's hand.

"Go and buy something you want."

"No, thank you," said Amy, as she gave it back. "It doesn't feel right to take money for helping someone."

Trish looked disappointed. So did Craig. "Maybe we can thank you some other way," he suggested. "I could take you and your family out sailing when the weather improves."

Amy liked that idea. Then she had another one that was even better. It was so good that it could solve everything. "There is something you could do," she said. "But we'll have to hurry if we're going to get there in time."

Craig grinned. "Let's go. You can explain what I have to do on the way."

Amy set off, with the singer striding along on one side of her and Trish on the other.

"Don't forget us," barked Hilton as he and Marmalade followed close behind.

By the time they reached the Primrose, there was a huge crowd of people waiting outside. Almost everyone on the Island was there. Even Plato had left his beloved television and come outside to watch the reopening ceremony.

None of them noticed the new arrivals. They were too busy watching Mom and Dad, who were standing beside the front door, looking very

nervous. Mom had a large pair of
scissors in her hand. Dad was holding
a microphone.

Amy jumped up and down at the
back of the crowd, waving her hand to
attract their attention. But neither of
them saw her.

Instead, Dad gave a small cough to clear his throat and started to speak. "Ladies and gentlemen. Thank you for coming here this morning to celebrate the reopening of the Primrose Tea Room."

While he talked, Amy wiggled her way through the crowd. She was almost at the front when Dad reached the last sentence of his speech. "I know you're all anxious to know the identity of our mystery celebrity..." He paused. Amy couldn't tell if he was trying to be dramatic, or if he was just trying to put off telling everyone the bad news.

Either way, the pause gave Amy the time she needed. As the crowd held its breath, waiting for the secret to be revealed, she ran forward and grabbed the microphone from Dad's hand.

Before he had a chance to take it back, she put the microphone to her mouth and started speaking. "Please welcome our mystery celebrity – Craig Redmile." Then she waved toward the back of the crowd where Craig was standing.

Everyone cheered and clapped when they saw him. They moved aside to let him through. Then they closed in again behind him, trying to get the best possible view. At the front of the crowd, old Mrs. Arnold waved her flag happily. She didn't seem at all disappointed that Craig wasn't the Queen.

Dad was too stunned to speak and Mom was too excited. She bounced up and down, waving the scissors in the air. Craig gently took them from her hand, cut the ribbon and declared the Primrose officially open. As the crowd cheered even louder, he took the microphone from Amy and started to sing.

The cheering died away as everyone settled down to enjoy the surprise concert. Hilton and the cats from the clan crept close to Amy. Plato flew over and perched on her shoulder, and Craig's cat joined them too.

"This is fantastic," said the parrot. "I must come outside more often."

Amy smiled. "The Primrose is

going to be a huge success after such a good start. And it would never have happened without Marmalade."

"My friends call me Mystery," purred the orange cat.

Amy Wild, Animal Talker

Collect all of Amy's fun, fur-filled adventures!

The Secret Necklace

Amy is thrilled to discover she can talk to animals!
But making friends is harder than she thought...

The Musical Mouse

There's a singing mouse at school! Can Amy find it
a new home before the principal catches it?

The Mystery Cat

Amy has to track down the owners of a playful orange
cat who's lost his home...and his memory.

The Furry Detectives

Things have been going missing on the Island and Amy
suspects there's an animal thief at work...

The Great Sheep Race

Will Amy train the Island's sheep in time for her
school fair's big fundraiser – a Great Sheep Race?

The Star-Struck Parrot

Amy gets to be an extra in a movie shot on the Island...
but can she help Plato the parrot land a part too?

The Lost Treasure

An ancient ring is discovered on the Island, sparking
a hunt for buried treasure...and causing chaos.

The Vanishing Cat

When one of the animals in the clan goes missing,
Amy faces her biggest mystery yet...